THE ODYSSEY

by
Homer

Student Packet

Written by
Gloria Levine, M. A.

Contains Masters for:

3	Prereading Activities
2	Literary Analysis Activities
1	Study Guide (121 questions)
1	Vocabulary Activity
4	Critical Thinking Activities
1	Study Guide for the Epic
5	Creative Writing Activities
2	Comprehension Quizzes (levels I and II)*
2	Unit Tests (levels I and II)*

PLUS   Detailed Answer Key

Level II quiz and test are for students with advanced skills

Note

The Laurel paperback edition of the book published by Dell was used to prepare this guide. The page references may differ in other editions.

Please note: Please assess the appropriateness of this book for the age level and maturity of your students prior to reading and discussing it with your class.

ISBN 1-56137-761-9

To order, contact your local school supply store, or—

Novel Units, Inc.
P.O. Box 97
Bulverde, TX 78163-0097

Web site: www.educyberstor.com

Name_____

Directions: With a partner, rate and discuss the following statements on a scale of 1-6. Keep these ratings in mind as you read the *Odyssey* and consider whether Homer and various characters in his poem feel the same way you do.

1 ———— 2 ———— 3 ———— 4 ———— 5 ———— 6

agree strongly   strongly disagree

Rating

____ 1. There's no place like home.
____ 2. Half the fun of going someplace lies in getting there.
____ 3. Revenge is sweet.
____ 4. Winning isn't everything; it's how you play the game that counts.
____ 5. Hell hath no fury like a woman scorned.
____ 6. All's fair in love and war.
____ 7. A man's home is his castle.
____ 8. The ends justify the means.
____ 9. Saving face is important to me.
____ 10. What goes around comes around.
____ 11. Good people usually get the reward they deserve.
____ 12. Life is hard.
____ 13. Real men don't eat quiche.
____ 14. Absence makes the heart grow fonder.
____ 15. A friend in need is a friend indeed.
____ 16. You should take care of yourself and your family first, then worry about saving the world.
____ 17. You should be willing to die for your country.
____ 18. If mothers and wives were in charge, there would be no war.
____ 19. You should express your anger.
____ 20. I'd rather be a live coward than a dead hero.
____ 21. Only the good die young.
____ 22. You shouldn't indulge freeloaders.
____ 23. Sometimes a little deceit is necessary.
____ 24. There's a lot of truth in many superstitions.
____ 25. Most people who give gifts want something in return.

Name_____

Allen Mandelbaum has translated the *Odyssey* from Greek to English. Even in the translation there are plenty of words that may be unfamiliar to you.

Directions

(A) Brainstorm possible definitions for these vocabulary words. (Make a wild guess if you have no idea.)

1. baldric (p. 233)
2. aegis (p. 42)
3. domineering (p. 115)
4. amphoras (p. 258)
5. chine (p. 287)
6. suppliant (p. 110)
7. libeccio (p. 51)
8. oracle (p. 261)
9. libations (p. 38)
10. concubine (p. 279)
11. augur (p. 28)
12. tempest (p. 140)
13. plunderers (p. 36)
14. estuary (p. 109)
15. grottoes (p. 3)
16. straits (p. 85)
17. sated (p. 288)
18. gluttony (p. 12)
19. clement (p. 103)
20. bard (p. 449)
21. booty (p. 44)
22. haversack (p. 103)
23. indolent (p. 115)
24. trident (p. 104)
25. partisans (p. 488)
26. astute (p. 120)
27. seer (p. 18)
28. steward (p. 8)
29. cairn (p. 475)
30. scepter (p. 24)
31. vagabonds (p. 277)
32. sagacity (p. 49)
33. insolent (p. 125)
34. chamberlain (p. 63)
35. obdurate (p. 462)
36. evasive (p. 74)
37. anvil (p. 154)
38. dexterous (p. 441)
39. torque (p. 371)

(B) Predict which box(es) each word belongs in and put the word there.

Eating/Drinking	Weather	People

Places	Good Human Qualities	Bad Human Qualities

(C) Trade papers with a partner and put an "X" by the definitions you think are correct before checking a dictionary. (How often did your partner manage to fool you despite his or her ignorance of the real meanings?)

(D) Circle the numbers of definitions that are accurate, according to the dictionary.

5

Name_____

The Odyssey
Study Questions
Use During Reading

Book One

1. What did Poseidon have against Odysseus?
2. Why did the goddess Athena want Zeus to send Hermes to Calypso?
3. What problems did Odysseus' absence cause for his wife and son?
4. Why did Telémachus go on a voyage?
5. "Long years ago, when she had just been touched by loveliness, Laértës purchased her." (p.18) Do you think Laértës' wife was jealous? For those who have read the Iliad: How was Laértës' extramarital behavior different from that of other husbands such as Agamemnon?
6. Prediction: Zeus mentioned that Agamemnon had been murdered by Aegísthus. Why do you suppose Agamemnon was killed?

Book Two

1. According to Antínoüs, why was Penelope to blame for the messy situation in Odysseus' house?
2. Who was Halithérses and what prediction did he make?
3. Athena disguised as Mentor told the suitors, "I am not incensed by all the suitor's plots and violence...Instead my wrath indicts the rest of you, who sit in silence." What was she saying?
4. Why didn't Eurycleia want Telémachus to leave?
5. Prediction: Will Telémachus' voyage be successful?

Book Three

1. Who killed Agamemnon and how was that murder avenged?
2. What did Nestor know about Odysseus' whereabouts?
3. Why did Nestor advise Telémachus to let Nestor's sons "guide (him) into sunlit Lacedaemon"? (p. 52)
4. What sort of sacrifice did Nestor oversee before sending his son off with Telémachus to Sparta?
5. Prediction: Will Telémachus follow in Oréstes' footsteps?

Book Four

1. What did Meneláus tell Telémachus about the wooden horse?
2. Why didn't Meneláus go right home after the Trojan War?
3. What did Meneláus reveal about Odysseus' whereabouts?
4. "Athena sent that phantom to the house of the divine Odysseus" (p. 90). Explain who Athena sent where—and why.
5. Prediction: Will the suitors attack Telémachus?

Book Five

1. How did Calypso help Odysseus leave the island—and why?
2. "Goddess, I know you've something else in mind—something beyond my being free to leave" (p. 100). What was probably Odysseus' tone of voice as he answered Calypso?
3. Why did Odysseus' boat sink?
4. Why didn't Odysseus drown?
5. Prediction: How will Odysseus be treated by the Phaeácians?

Book Six

1. Why did Nausícaa go to the riverbank?
2. "...terrified, they scattered on the shore, one here, one there" (p. 120) Who? Why?
3. "Would that my husband were a man like him" (p. 124) What was Nausícaa thinking?
4. What did Nausícaa instruct Odysseus to do—and why?
5. Prediction: Will the Phaeácians help Odysseus?

Book Seven

1. For what skills were Phaeácian men and women known?
2. How was Odysseus treated when he reached the palace?
3. "So profound is her good sense that—for those men and women she esteems— she acts as judge in feuds and bickerings." (p. 133) Who was "she"?
4. Why did Arétë ask Odysseus about his cloak?
5. Prediction: Do you think Alcínoüs will press Odysseus further to marry his daughter?

Book VIII

1. Briefly describe the three stories sung by Demódocus.
2. Cite the passage where Euryalus taunted Odysseus.
3. List the contests held by the Phaeácians.
4. At which event did Odysseus excel?
5. Prediction: Will Odysseus tell the truth about who he is and where he has been?

Book IX

1. Briefly describe the dangers faced by Odysseus' men in their travels—and how they fared, in each case.

Danger	Description	Outcome
Cíconës		
Lotus-Eaters		
Cyclops		

2. Why did Odysseus and his men go into the Cyclops' cave?
3. "This is the gift I give to you, my guest" (p. 180) Why didn't Odysseus ever receive that gift—and why wouldn't he have appreciated it if he had?
4. Why didn't the other Cyclops help Polyphémus when he cried out after being blinded by Odysseus?
5. Prediction: Will Poseidon ever get the chip off his shoulder and stop tormenting Odysseus?

Book X

1. What gift—and instructions—did Aeolus give Odysseus?
2. How did Odysseus and his men end up back in Aeólia?
3. How did the Laestrygónians treat Odysseus and his men?
4. "Its root was black; its flower was white as milk. It's moly for the gods" (p. 200). Who gave Odysseus that gift and what was it for?
5. Prediction: Why will Odysseus return to the island where Circe lives?

Book XI
1. Who were the first three people Odysseus met in Hades?
2. "It was lament for you—your gentleness and wisdom...—that robbed me of the honey-sweet of life" (p. 219). What did Odysseus' mother mean?
3. What did Tirésias predict?
4. List three Greeks in Hades who had fought alongside of Odysseus in the Trojan war.
5. Prediction: Odysseus' mother describes her husband as lying sorrowfully, in rags. Will Odysseus ever see him again?

Book XII
1. Why did Odysseus put wax in the crew's ears?
2. What danger did Odysseus face after passing the Sirens?
3. How did Odysseus' men get into trouble on the island of the sun god? How many survived?
4. "For nine days I was dragged; and on the tenth the gods cast me upon Ogygia's coast" (p. 251) Who did Odysseus meet there?
5. Prediction: What new problems will Odysseus have on his trip to Ithaca?

Book XIII
1. How did Odysseus end up back in Ithaca, sleeping on the beach?
2. Why were the Phaeácians punished—and how?
3. "So everything seemed strange to one who was the ruler of this land" (p. 261) Why?
4. How did Athena disguise Odysseus and where did she send him?
5. Prediction: Who will be the first to recognize Odysseus?

Book XIV
1. Who was Eumáeus and what did he think of the suitors?
2. Did Odysseus tell Eumáeus the same tale about his past that he had told the Alcínoüs and Arétë?
3. What did the swineherd mean when he told the stranger that "vagabonds have far more need of food and shelter than of truth" (p. 277)?
4. How did the stranger get Eumáeus to give him a cloak?
5. Prediction: Will Odysseus reveal himself to his son right away?

Book XV
1. Why did Telémachus return home to Ithaca?
2. What two omens arise are described in this book?
3. What plans did Odysseus and his son make?
4. "...here, with his wealth, Laértës bought me—and so I came to see this land" (p. 311) How did the swineherd get "here"?
5. Prediction: How will the suitors treat the tattered stranger?

Book XVI
1. Who was the first person Telémachus went to see on his return to Ithaca?
2. Briefly describe the reunion of Telémachus and his father.
3. Penelope reminded whom that "your father came to this house a fugitive, in fear of all the Ithacans" (p. 331)? Why?
4. How was Eurymachus deceitful?
5. Prediction: How will Penelope treat the tattered stranger?

Book XVII
1. Who was Theoclymenus and what did he have to say about Odysseus?
2. Why did Odysseus feel like beating up Melánthius?
3. "But Argos, just as soon as he had seen his master after nineteen years, fell prey to death's dark fate" (p. 348). Explain what happened in two or three words.
4. Who was the only suitor not to give Odysseus food or gifts? What did he do instead?
5. Prediction: Will Penelope's interpretation of the "sign of the sneeze" prove correct?

Book XVIII
1. Why did Irus challenge Odysseus—then try to run away?
2. Why did Odysseus warn Amphínomus to leave the house?
3. List three of the gifts the suitors gave Penelope.
4. "I'll fetch Telémachus, who'll hack you into bits." (p. 372) Who was Odysseus mad at—and why?
5. Prediction: Will Odysseus spare any of the suitors?

10

Name_____

Book XIX
1. How did the suitors find out about Penelope's scheme?
2. "I saw Odysseus there, he was my guest" (p. 385). How did the stranger convince Penelope that this was true?
3. How did Eurycleia recognize Odysseus?
4. What test did Penelope devise for the suitors?
5. Prediction: Which suitor will Odysseus kill first?

Book XX
1. Where does Homer tell us that Odysseus had his doubts about whether he could succeed against the suitors—and escape the vengeance of their families?
2. Why was Odysseus happy to hear the thunder and the woman's comment?
3. "Sad man! He has the likeness of a king" (p. 409). Who made this observation—and what did he mean?
4. Why did Amphínomous suggest they give up the murder plan?
5. Prediction: What sort of sign will Odysseus give Telémachus when it is time to fight?

Book XXI
1. What did Penelope promise if the tattered stranger succeeded in shooting the arrow through the axes?
2. Did anyone succeed at the archery test?
3. Besides Telémachus, who knew the stranger's identity?
4. "That said, he gave the signal with his brows" (p. 434). What signal?
5. Prediction: What will happen to the women who insulted or were disloyal to Odysseus?

11

Book XXII

1. Why did Eurymachus offer to have the suitors "gather through the land your recompense for all that we have drunk and eaten in your halls" (p. 438)?
2. How did the suitors arm themselves?
3. What two men did Odysseus spare?
4. What happened to the handmaidens identified by Eurycleia?
5. Prediction: How will the stranger convince Penelope he is Odysseus?

Book XXIII

1. Why did Penelope say, "Dear nurse...the gods have led your wits astray" (p. 457)?
2. Why did Odysseus tell the servants to dance and feast?
3. How did Odysseus convince Penelope it was really he?
4. Where did Odysseus go the morning after his reunion with Penelope?
5. Prediction: How will Laértës react when he sees his son?

Book XXIV

1. Whom did Hermes lead to Hades?
2. What was the "uncanny dread" Laértës felt after his reunion with Odysseus? (p. 484)
3. Why did Eupeithes and others go to Laértës' farm?
4. Who was slain by Laértës?
5. Who convinced Odysseus to "halt now; have done with this relentless war"? (p. 491)

Your Mythology IQ

From the myths and fairy tales you have read, the stories you've heard and the cartoons you've watched, you have probably picked up a lot of information about Greek gods and goddesses. Several gods and goddesses make an appearance in the *Odyssey*. Some of these didn't acquire the reputation you may know about until people after Homer told stories about them. (For instance, Achilles didn't have his problematic heel in the *Odyssey*.)

Match each of the names on the left with the description you think fits best.

___	1. Zeus	A.	god of war
___	2. Amphitrítë	B.	supreme god of the Greeks
___	3. Apollo	C.	goddess of the sea
___	4. Poseidon	D.	god of archery, music and prophecy
___	5. Arës	E.	goddess of wisdom
___	6. Aphrodítë	F.	lame god of metal-working
___	7. Artemis	G.	god of sea and earthquakes
___	8. Hermes	H.	goddess of hunting
___	9. Athena	I.	goddess of love and beauty
___	10. Hephéastus	J.	messenger of the gods; guide for the dead
___	11. Hélios	K.	queen of the kingdom of the dead
___	12. Perséphonë	L.	sun god

Your Mythology IQ

Scoring:

9–12	Holy cow! You know your gods and goddesses.
6–9	Your standing on Mt. Olympus is a little shaky.
less than 6	You are about to make a lot of new acquaintances in high places.

Name_____

Directions: You can use pictures graphics (pictures and symbols) to help you remember "who's who" in the *Odyssey*.

Here is a list of some characters in Book One of the *Odyssey*: **Odysseus, Calypso, Poseidon, Zeus, Telémachus, Penelope, Athena**

As you read the poem fill in the story map below with each character's name and a symbol or drawing that represents that character. Map other books on other pieces of paper.

Book One

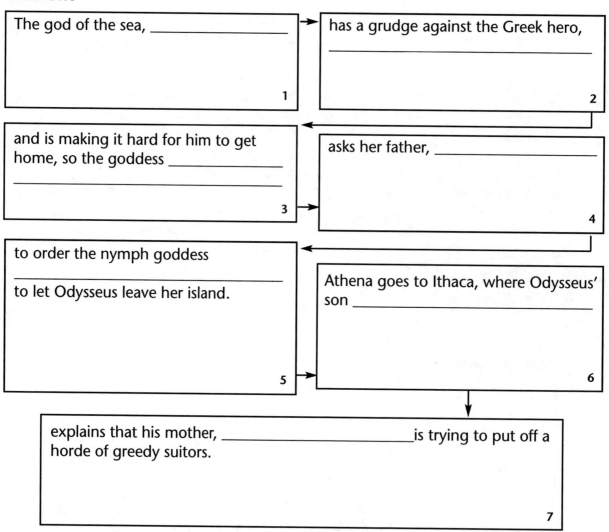

The god of the sea, _____ → has a grudge against the Greek hero, _____   **1**   **2**

and is making it hard for him to get home, so the goddess _____   **3**   ← asks her father, _____   **4**

to order the nymph goddess _____ to let Odysseus leave her island.   **5**   ← Athena goes to Ithaca, where Odysseus' son _____   **6**

explains that his mother, _____is trying to put off a horde of greedy suitors.   **7**

14

Directions: You are Nausícaa. You decide to write to a newspaper columnist about a man you have just met.

Step 1: Finish the letter begun for you, below:

Dear Gabby,

I have enjoyed your column for years—especially your counsel on matters of the heart. I never thought I would be writing to you about my own lovelife, but I need some advice. Plenty of men are interested in me, but _____

_____

_____Finally I've met someone who is

_____

My parents _____. The only problem is

_____

_____I know you may say that I hardly know him, but

_____

and now he is about to leave town. What should I do?

Signed,

Frustrated Phaeacian

Step 2: In small group, brainstorm possible advice Gabby might give to Nausícaa. Weigh the pros and cons of each. (A chart for organizing your ideas is shown below.) Then write a letter of advice to Nausícaa, using details from the completed chart.

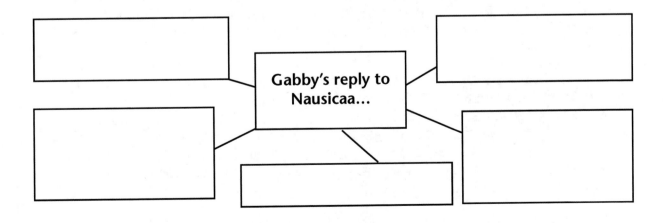

Gabby's reply to Nausicaa...

Name_____

Directions: Write a character sketch of Odysseus (or Laértës, or any other character of your choice from the *Odyssey*). The finished sketch should be a brief, vivid description that includes physical characteristics—appearance, surroundings—and personality.

Prewriting
1. Imagine Odysseus (or the character you choose) at a particular point in the story. Get together in a small group to brainstorm a list of his characteristics.
   - How would you describe his eyes? his face? his hair? Is he tall? short? What are his hands and feet like? Does he have any distinguishing marks? What does his usual facial expression tell you about his personality?
   - How would you describe his posture? the way he moves? What is his voice like? How does he speak? What is his usual tone of voice—when speaking to Calypso? to his men? to Telémachus? to Penelope? How is he dressed? What does his clothing tell you about his personality and situation?
   - What other details about Odysseus spring to mind? What responsibilities does he have? What does he like to do with his free time? What are his dreams and fears? How does he feel about himself?
   - What do you know about Odysseus' family and background? What else do you imagine? What was his relationship with his mother and father like when he was a child? What was his early married life like? How did he interact with his young son? How do his family members feel about him now? What does he value? How does he feel about life?
2. Focus on the most "telling" details from #1, above. Which of the details will help you, the writer, convey a single, strong impression of what Odysseus is like? Circle these.

Writing: Choose one of the following ways to give the reader a single, focused impression of Odysseus (approximately 250 words):
   a. Pretend that you are someone who knows Odysseus well, such as Laértës or Penelope. Someone who doesn't know Odysseus has asked for your impression of him.
   b. Write a short story about Odysseus. The story might focus on an incident in Ithaca before the Trojan War, something that happened during the war, or something that occurred during one of his trials (on Circe's or Calypso's island, for instance).

Postwriting: Read the character sketch aloud to your editing group. Make sure that it "sounds right." Is there a nice variety of long and short sentences? Do the words "flow" as you read the sketch aloud? Have you avoided unintentional repetition of words and phrases? Ask for suggestions about how to make the sequence of events more clear or how to give the reader a sharper picture of Odysseus. Revise your draft, incorporating some of these suggestions. Proofread the sketch carefully for correct grammar and punctuation.

Collect the group's character sketches into a printed booklet.

16

Directions: Write a poem from Polyphémus' point of view.

Prewriting
1. Reread Book IX, in which the Cyclops is described.
2. Discuss these questions with a partner or in small group.
   - What does the Cyclops look like?
   - How does he spend his time?
   - What sort of personality does he have?
   - How does he treat Odysseus and his men?
   - Did they have the right to enter his cave?
   - How did Odysseus escape?
   - Do you feel at all sorry for him?
   - How did he find out Odysseus' name?
3. Close your eyes and imagine that you are Polyphémus. You come back to your cave and what do you find? How do you feel? What do you see? What do the men do and say? What is your response? You fall asleep. What wakes you up? What is the pain like? Why are you enraged? What do you think? What do you remember? What happens next? Why doesn't anyone help you? How do Odysseus and the others escape? How do you feel? Odysseus gives his "parting shot." What passes through your mind? Odysseus and his men are gone now. You return to your cave and sit down. How do you feel? What memories pass through your mind? What plans do you make?

Writing
4. Pick up a pen (or sit at the computer) and begin your poem.
5. Read your poem aloud and try to cut out all unnecessary words. Play with different line breaks until the poem "sounds right" to you. Add some rhyme, repeated sounds, and/or repeated images if you like.

After Writing
6. Read your poem to your writing group. Have them share which lines they particularly like—and tell why.
7. Have them share how the poem makes them feel about Polyphémus. Does he disgust them? anger them? frighten them? Do you feel sorry for him?
8. Read "Polyphémus Revisited" by Sallie Hughes Scott, English Journal, NCTE, January 1996, page 40.

Name_____

Project: Create a duologue (two-person conversation) that reveals two characters' views of Odysseus. Assume that your audience is composed of a group of high school students assigned the *Odyssey*.

Prewriting
1. Choose one of these pairs:
   - Telémachus and Polyphémus
   - Penelope and Calypso
   - Nausícaa and Círcë
   - Antínoüs and Eumáeus
   - Eurycleia and Melántho
   - Poseidon and Athena
2. Students who have selected the same pairs discuss the characters' relationships with Odysseus, then improvise conversations that the two might have about Odysseus. Record on audiotape.
3. After the improvisations, students listen to the tape and discuss ad-libbed lines that seemed particularly appropriate to the character, effective, or insightful. Group members suggest additional comments characters might have made.

During Writing
4. As you write your duologues, keep these questions in mind-
   - **Voice:** What am I like? How do I sound? What tone do I use? What sort of language do I use? What is my attitude toward my subject—Odysseus—and toward the other speaker?
   - **Audience:** Who is the reader? What help does the reader need to understand my statements?
   - **Purpose:** Why am I having this conversation about Odysseus? How will I let the audience know the situation in which the discussion takes place? Am I arguing with the other person about something? Am I trying to make a decision? to figure something out? to influence the other person?
   - **Content:** What is my relationship to Odysseus? How did I meet him? How does he feel about me? How do I feel about him? What do I like about him? What don't I like? Does anything about him puzzle me? What do I think about the way he is being forced to undergo all these trials? What values do we share? What differences do we have?

After Writing
5. With a partner, read your duologue to a group of fellow students (who have selected other pairs of characters for their duologues). (You might do this as Reader's Theater, with simple costumes, props, and gesturing as you read.)

Directions: First, in a small group talk about the relationships between Odysseus and the women in the chart below. Label each arrow with a brief description of the relationship.

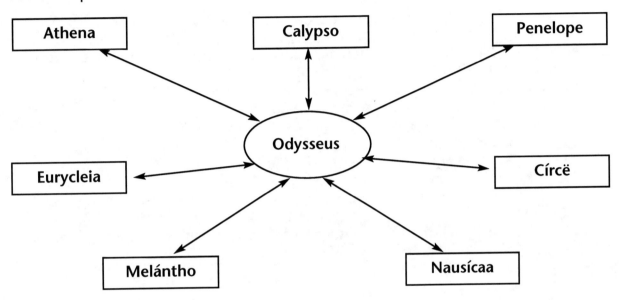

Next, write a five-paragraph essay that supports this thesis:

The view of women presented by Homer in the *Odyssey* reveals a great deal about attitudes toward women in ancient Greece.

Paragraph One should state the thesis and present three points in support of that thesis.
Paragraph Two should explain point #1 and provide reasons or examples from the story.
Paragraph Three should explain point #2.
Paragraph Four should explain point #3.
Paragraph Five should restate the thesis and summarize the three points.

In choosing your three points, consider these questions: For what qualities does Odysseus value women? What sorts of decisions do these women make? How does Odysseus feel threatened by some of the women in the *Odyssey*? What seems to motivate these women? What are their strengths and weaknesses? Is Athena being portrayed as the "perfect woman"? How do each of the others compare with Athena? Is Odysseus closer to Athena than he is to Penelope? Does Odysseus consider all of these women to be subservient to himself?

Name_____

Directions: There are many insults and gory descriptions in the *Odyssey*. Here are a few—

Insults:

The gods indeed may teach brash blustering to you and braggart speech. (p. 16)

You...are a rabble-rousing lout. (p. 31)

Nothing is more obscene, more bestial, than a woman's mind when it is all intent on dregs. (p. 227)

You arrogant and vicious... and yet you are a sham, Madman...(p. 331)

...it takes a filthy wretch to lead a filthy wretch...this repugnant pest...that laggard...to scrounge and lounge—that's all his avid belly wants (p. 344)

...you reckless orator (p. 351)

You are just a brash and brazen beggar. (p. 352)

Your wits don't match your beauty. (p. 352)

How glib he is—this wretch; he gabs as if he were a clacking, oven-tending hag. (p.361)

You scrubby foreigner, brash, unabashed...Are you wild with wine or do you always babble with muddled mind? (p. 372)

Arrogant slut (p. 382)

Gore Descriptions:

when his maw was stuffed with human flesh (p. 178)

They speared my comrades, carried them like fish—an obscene meal. (p. 195)

Face down, along the ground, my chest pierced through, lifting my fists, dying, I beat the earth. (p. 227)

Scylla swallowed them as, in their horrid struggle, my dear friends stretched out to me their hands... (p. 245)

it crushed his skull (p. 250)

The point passed through and out the tender neck...mortal blood gushed from his nostrils...(p. 437)

1. What is your favorite insult in the *Odyssey*? (Cite Book, page, and first few words.)

   _____

2. Who do you think meets the must gruesome end in the *Odyssey*? (Name character, cite Book and page.)

   _____

3. Pretend that you are a character in the *Odyssey* and make up an insult worthy of Homer.

   Character _____ Who are you insulting?_____

   Why?_____

   Insult: _____

   _____

Name_____

Directions: Many of the characters and events in the *Odyssey* have modern-day counterparts—in life, fiction, or art. For instance, you might see a similarity between one of Odysseus' trials (e.g., The Sirens) and the dilemmas faced by various politicians. (Do I do what I think is right—or listen to the voices of special-interest groups who will contribute money to my campaign?) Or you might see a resemblance between the travails of Homer Simpson and Odysseus, or similarities between Calypso's loss of Odysseus and Jacques Cousteau's recent loss of his boat, *The Calypso*. (If you're feeling creative, draw a cartoon that captures the *Odyssey*-like nature of the present-day situation.)

Odyssey Situation	Present-Day Situation	How They Are Alike
Odysseus' thwarted desire to return home		
the Sirens		
Scylla and Charybdis		
Agamemnon's murder		
conflict between Telémachus and suitors		
Poseidon's revenge		
the killing of the suitors		
the portents		
the ghosts		
various places in the *Odyssey* (e.g. the island of the Cyclops, the Land of the Laestrygónians, Circe's island, etc.)		

Name_____

Directions: Lawrence Kohlberg evolved a model of moral development to explain what motivates an individual to act as he or she does. Kohlberg believes that his model can be applied to individuals of any culture. There are six levels of moral development in his model. All people do not reach the highest levels.

Decide which level best describes each character by the end of the poem.

Level I   Acts to avoid pain or punishment.
Level II   Acts to get a reward.
Level III   Acts to gain approval.
Level IV   Acts because of belief in the law.
Level V   Acts for the welfare of others.
Level VI   Acts because of a self-formulated set of principles

Character	Level	Reason
Odysseus		
Athena		
Calypso		
Polyphémus		
Penelope		
Telémachus		
Eumáeus		
Melántho		
Melánthius		
Alcínoüs		
Arétë		
Nausícaa		
Antínoüs		
Agamemnon		
Poseidon		
Irus		
Eurycleia		

Name_____

Directions: Several characters in the *Odyssey* are faced with important decisions. Help them make these decisions by creating decision-making grids. A grid for Poseidon is started below. Add another choice Poseidon had, and two more criteria for measuring each choice. Then rate each choice by the "criteria" questions at the top of each chart (1=yes; 2=no; 3=maybe). On separate paper, make additional decision-making grids for two of the other questions at the bottom of the page. Finally, choose one of the decisions and write an essay about the decision. (What was the decision? Why was it important? What choices did (s)he have? Did (s)he make the best decision? Why or why not?)

Problem: What should Poseidon do when he learns that Odysseus has blinded his son?

Possible Choices ↓	Criteria			
	Will I get revenge?	Will I anger the other gods?		
Kill Odysseus.				
Make Odysseus suffer: keep him from getting home.				

Questions for Additional Charts:
1. What should Telémachus do about those pesky suitors?
2. What should Odysseus do about Elpénor?
3. How should Odysseus escape from Polyphémus?
4. What should Odysseus do when the ship passes the Sirens?
5. What should Penelope do about the suitors?

Directions: The *Odyssey* is considered one of the most important **folk epics**. An **epic** is a long narrative poem in elevated style presenting heroic characters in a series of adventures. This activity is designed to acquaint you with some of the characteristics and devices found in many epic poems: *invocation of the muse, in media res, Homeric similes, grand style, vast setting, courageous action, supernatural forces,* and *epithets*.

I. **Invocation of the Muse:** The Muses are daughters of Zeus, goddesses of the fine arts who provide creative inspiration. Most epic poems open by stating the theme and invoking a Muse to inspire and instruct the poet. What does Homer ask the Muse to do at the beginning of the *Odyssey*?

II. **In media res:** Many epic poems begin "in the middle of the action." The *Odyssey* begins in the midst of what situation?

III. **Homeric simile/grand style:** A **simile** is a comparison between two things, and often contains the words "like" or "as." (*Example:* My hands are like ice.) The **Homeric simile** refers to an **epic simile**, an unusually elaborate comparison, that extends through a number of lines:
   "Just as a lion is beset by doubt and fear when he's surrounded by a crowd of hunters closing in—a cunning ring—so was Penelope, while pondering, beset." (Book IV, pp. 89-90)
   A. Find the simile, below, in the text. Explain what two things are being compared—and how they are alike.
   "And even as the Archer Artemis...just so... Nausícaa..." (Book VI, pp. 118-119)

   _____ is like _____ because both

   _____.

   B. Cite three other **Homeric similes** (by Book and page number and the first few words of the first line) found in the *Odyssey*. Put a star by your favorite one.

   _____

   _____

   _____

C. Look for the longest simile you can find in the *Odyssey* and cite the lines here:

D. Give a literal paraphrase of that passage, using as few words as possible.

E. Share your simile and paraphrase with a partner.

F. Compose your own Homeric simile to describe one of the following

a fight with your sibling
a crowd you've been part of
a time you ran away from something

a frightening or lovely sound
an inspiring view you recently saw
something that caused you discomfort or pain

IV. **Vast setting:** As you can see by looking at the map that precedes the poem, the setting of the story covers a lot of territory. List six places visited by Odysseus before he arrives home in Ithaca:

1.
2.
3.
4.
5.
6.

V. **Courageous Action:** Epic poems contain legendary heroes engaged in courageous actions. Describe three courageous actions performed by Odysseus.

1.
2.
3.

Name_____

VI. **Supernatural Forces:** In most epic poems, there are supernatural forces such as gods, angels, and demons who interest themselves in the action and even step in from time to time. Provide three examples of this in the *Odyssey*.
1.
2.
3.

VII. **Homeric Epithet:** An **epithet** is an adjectival phrase so often repeated in connection with a person or thing that it almost becomes a part of the name, as "wily Odysseus," "faithful Eurycleia," and "wise Penelope."

A. Create three newspaper headlines, based on events in the *Odyssey*, that incorporate Homerian epithets.
Sample: Wily Odysseus Eludes Sirens

1.
2.
3.

B. Create an **epitaph** for one of the dead suitors. Include the suitor's **epithet** in the epitaph.
Sample: Melánthius: The goatherd—king of insults—
has gone to his final rest.
He could badger, bait and jibe
along with the very best.

_____
_____
_____
_____
_____

C. Try your hand at writing pithy epithets for each of the following:

the President
the governor of your state
a current military dictator
a U.S. general
your favorite cartoon character
a character on TV
a movie role
your favorite athlete
your favorite actor
a political figure you admire
a political figure you dislike
your parent
your favorite teacher
your best friend
your employer
your neighbor
someone who has been in the news a lot lately
the Time magazine "person of the year"
the ABC "person of the week"
YOURSELF
your ideal self
someone else of your choice

Identification: Match each name on the left with the proper description on the right.

____ 1. Homer
____ 2. Calypso
____ 3. Odysseus
____ 4. Athena
____ 5. Telémachus
____ 6. Penelope
____ 7. Antínoüs
____ 8. Nausícaa
____ 9. Alcínoüs
____ 10. Polyphémus
____ 11. Circe
____ 12. Sirens

A. Enchantress who changed Odysseus' crew into pigs
B. Odysseus' wife
C. Sea nymph who kept Odysseus on her island for eight years
D. Goddess, daughter of Zeus, who is Odysseus' close friend
E. Author of the *Odyssey*
F. Maidens whose singing lures passing sailors to their deaths
G. Odysseus' son
H. Generous, kind king of the Phaeacians
I. Smart, courageous Greek hero of the *Odyssey*
J. Cyclops blinded by Odysseus
K. Evil leader of the suitors
L. Innocent, virtuous daughter of Alcínoüs

True/False: Label each statement T (true) or F (false). (For bonus points, rewrite false statements on the back of the paper to make them true.)

____ 13. Athena, as Méntës, advised Telémachus to search for news of his father.
____ 14. Penelope told the suitors that she would never remarry.
____ 15. Agamemnon was killed in the Trojan war by Menaláus.
____ 16. The suitors planned to ambush and kill Telémachus.
____ 17. Poseidon was angry with Odysseus for blinding the god's son.
____ 18. Odysseus met Nausícaa on a beach after he nearly drowned.
____ 19. Alcínoüs told Odysseus he would help him if Odysseus promised to marry Nausícaa.
____ 20. Odysseus pretended that he could not throw the discus very far at the Phaeácians' tournament.
____ 21. Odysseus told the Phaeácians a false tale about his past.
____ 22. Circe turned Odysseus into a pig.
____ 23. Odysseus met the ghost of his dead mother in Hades.
____ 24. Odysseus' men angered the sun god by eating his cattle.

Matching: Match each cause with its effect.

CAUSES	EFFECTS
__ 25. Odysseus told the kind Phaeácians he needed help to get home.	A. Zeus agreed to send Hermes to Calypso with a message.
__ 26. Nestor advised Telémachus to go to Sparta.	B. Antínoüs denied all guilt and blamed Penelope.
__ 27. Elpénor fell off a roof as Odysseus and his men were hurrying away.	C. Odysseus' son went to see Meneláus.
__ 28. Telémachus criticized the suitors for wasting his father's wealth.	D. He returned home years after the end of the war.
__ 29. Athena asked her father to help free Odysseus.	E. He did not drown.
__ 30. Odysseus plugged his crewmen's ears with wax.	F. Nausícaa's handmaidens ran off in fear.
__ 31. Odysseus was filthy and covered with brine.	G. The king and queen agreed to provide Odysseus with a crew.
__ 32. The bard told the tale of how the Greeks hid in the wooden horse.	H. Odysseus wept.
__ 33. The greedy crew thought the bag of winds contained gold, and opened it.	I. The forgetful men had to be dragged back to their ship.
__ 34. Odysseus' men ate some fruit in the land of the Lotus-Eaters.	J. A hurricane blew them back to Aeólia.
__ 35. A nymph gave Odysseus a magic shawl.	K. His ghost begged Odysseus to give him a proper burial.
__ 36. A wind had blown Meneláus to Egypt, where the gods held him.	L. They were immune to the music and passed safely by the reefs.

29

Name_____

Directions: Several incidents that appear in the first 12 books of the *Odyssey* are listed below. Choose ten of these, and summarize each one in one short paragraph. Be sure to include details that explain how the character(s) came to be in the situation and to mention any decisions or outcomes that resulted from the incident you are summarizing. (Use separate paper to write your paragraphs.)

1. Athena gave Telémachus some advice regarding the suitors.
2. Telémachus appeared before the elders of Ithaca.
3. Old Nestor told Telémachus what he knew of the end of the Trojan War and the fates of the warriors.
4. Penelope's sister visited her and soothed her.
5. Odysseus was freed by Calypso and ran into trouble.
6. Odysseus met Nausícaa.
7. Odysseus went to the palace of Alcínoüs and Arété.
8. Odysseus attended the feast of the Phaeácians.
9. Odysseus and his men visited the Cyclops' cave.
10. Odysseus and his men spent time on Circe's island.
11. Odysseus met the seer Tirésias in Hades.
12. Odysseus and his men visited the island of the sun-god.

Identification: Find the description on the right that matches the character on the left. Write the letter of the description next to the matching number.

____	1. Odysseus	A.	disloyal, insulting serving maid
____	2. Eumáeus	B.	faithful old nurse
____	3. Penelope	C.	Odysseus' wife
____	4. Telémachus	D.	hero of the *Odyssey*
____	5. Melánthius	E.	loyal old cowherd
____	6. Eurycleia	F.	traitorous goatherd
____	7. Zeus	G.	Odysseus' friend; Athena's disguise
____	8. Mentor	H.	supreme god
____	9. Philóetius	I.	Odysseus' son
____	10. Melántho	J.	faithful swineherd

Multiple Choice: Choose the BEST answer.

____ 11. In order to punish the Phaeácians for helping Odysseus
    A. Zeus smashed their ship to bits.
    B. Zeus visited a plague on the Phaeácian people.
    C. Poseidon turned their ship to stone.
    D. Poseidon wrapped the city in a fog.

____ 12. When Odysseus got to Ithaca, Athena disguised him as
    A. a beggar
    B. a merchant
    C. a bard
    D. a herald

____ 13. Eumáeus ended up in Ithaca after he was
    A. purchased as a slave by Antínoüs
    B. kidnapped by a slave who cared for him
    C. turned into a swineherd by Circe
    D. stranded there as punishment by Poseidon

_____ 14. The first Ithacan to whom Odysseus revealed his true identity was
A. Laértës
B. Eumáeus
C. Penelope
D. Telémachus

_____ 15. Melánthius insulted and kicked Odysseus because Melánthius
A. did not want any competitors in his begging business
B. wanted to discourage Odysseus from courting Penelope
C. was jealous of Odysseus after his display of strength
D. was just plain nasty

_____ 16. Odysseus beat Irus after Irus
A. challenged him to a boxing match
B. kicked Odysseus' dog
C. threw a stool at Odysseus
D. insulted Penelope

_____ 17. When faithful Eurycleia recognized Odysseus, he
A. embraced her and wept
B. kissed her feet
C. winked and sneezed to signal her to keep his secret
D. threatened to kill her if she revealed his identity

_____ 18. Together Odysseus and Telémachus came up with a plan to
A. lock the suitors out of the palace
B. kill the suitors
C. set Telémachus up as King of Ithaca
D. return Laértës to his position as king

_____ 19. Penelope told the suitors she would marry the one who could pass her test of skill at _____
A. archery
B. discuss throw
C. javelin toss
D. boxing

____ 20. The first suitor to die was
   A. Medon
   B. Mentor
   C. Antínoüs
   D. Melántho

____ 21. After the slaughter of the suitors, Odysseus proposed that everyone dance and make merry to
   A. delay outsiders from discovering the killings
   B. celebrate Odysseus' revenge
   C. celebrate Telémachus' wedding
   D. delay Penelope from discovering his identity

____ 22. If Athena and Zeus hadn't stepped in at the end,
   A. all the suitors would have been killed
   B. more blood would have been shed in the fight between Odysseus' party and the families of the suitors
   C. the treacherous handmaidens would have been hanged
   D. Laértës and Odysseus would have been killed by Eupeithes

Fill-Ins: Fill in each blank with a word from the list.

loom	Cyclops	roof	scar
axheads	spared	boat	songs
beggar	bed	bard	kill
laundry	swine	dog	Eurymachus
eagles	thunderbolt		

23. Odysseus' crewman, Elpénor, got drunk and fell off a _____.

24. Athena disguised Odysseus as a _____ so that he could carry out his plans to punish the suitors.

25. Calypso wanted Odysseus to stay, but she helped him build a _____.

26. Nausícaa and her handmaidens met Odysseus after going to the river to do _____.

27. Maybe Homer was thinking of himself when he described Demódocus, the blind
    _____.

28. Odysseus wept when he saw his faithful_____Argos raise his head and
    die.

29. When Athena ordered the fighting to stop, Zeus cast down a
    _____ to let everyone know he was behind her.

30. Some of Penelope's traitorous maids revealed that she was deliberately undoing
    her work at the _____ each night.

31. When Polyphémus cried out in pain, the other _____ thought he
    was crazy because he said "No-one" was there.

32. Circe turned Odysseus' men into _____.

33. The old nurse recognized Odysseus by his _____.

34. Several times in the story, the appearance of a fierce _____
    was interpreted as a sign that Odysseus would get revenge.

35. Penelope finally believed that the stranger was Odysseus when he revealed that he
    knew something special about the _____.

36. In order to test the suitors, Penelope lined up twelve _____.

37. Odysseus had his men tie him to the mast so that he wouldn't be drawn to his
    death by certain alluring _____.

38. Melántho disgusted Odysseus with her attentions to
    _____.

39. The swineherd and cowherd helped _____ the suitors.

40. Phémius and Medon were _____.

Short Answer: Write your answers in complete sentences

1. How and why did Poseidon punish the Phaeácian seamen?

2. How and why did Athena disguise Odysseus when he arrived in Ithaca?

3. How did Eumáeus the swineherd end up living in Ithaca?

4. Why did Odysseus quickly reveal his true identity to his son—and his son, only?

5. How did Melánthius the goatherd provoke the disguised Odysseus—and how did Odysseus get revenge later?

6. Who was Irus and what was the outcome of his altercation with Odysseus?

7. How did Eurycleia recognize Odysseus—and what was his reaction?

8. What sort of plan did Odysseus and Telémachus make for dealing with the problematic suitors?

9. What test did Penelope devise for the suitors, and who passed it?

10. In the fight with the suitors, who did Odysseus kill first—and why?

11. How did Odysseus try to delay Ithacans outside the palace from learning of the killings—and why?

12. How did the fighting between Odysseus' group and the suitors' families and supporters end?

13. **Welcome Home Banner:** Pretend that you are responsible for printing up the one-sentence banner that the loyal Ithacans will put up over the palace doors when Odysseus resumes his king-ship. What will it say?

_____

Chart: Theme
The themes of wisdom and foolishness are developed throughout the *Odyssey*. In each box, below, briefly explain how the situation is a demonstration of wisdom and/or foolishness—and how the experience results in personal growth.

---

14. Odysseus and his men encounter Polyphémus.

---

15. Odysseus and his men encounter the Sirens.

---

16. Odysseus and his men encounter Scylla and Charybdis.

---

17. Odysseus' men open the bag of winds.

---

18. Odysseus and his men stay on Helios' island.

Quote Identification: Identify the speaker in each case and put his/her statement into your own words.

> "The wind that carried me from Ilion brought me to Ismarus, the Cíconës. I sacked their city, massacred their men."

19. Speaker:
20. Own words:

> "I am too weak too check their insolence; yes—even if I tried, I lack warcraft, the power that defies. Had I the force, I certainly would fight."

21. Speaker:
22. Own words:

"Dear heart, don't rage: Odysseus, let the wisdom you've displayed in all else show here now. It is the gods who destined us to sorrow; they begrudged our staying side by side—the two of us—enjoying youth and coming to the start of our old age together."

23. Speaker:
24. Own words:

"But I was not allowed to sate my eyes, to see my own beloved son: my wife denied that sight to me—she killed me first."

25. Speaker:
26. Own words:

"Laértës' son, Odysseus, sprung from Zeus, o man of many wiles, this is too much. Halt now; have done with this relentless war, lest you provoke the wrath of Zeus, the lord of thunder, he whose voice is carried far."

27. Speaker:
28. Own words:

Essay: (Choose three.) Each essay should include at least three examples or reasons taken directly from the *Odyssey* as supportive evidence.

  A. Describe three of the places visited by Odysseus. In each case, describe how the setting drives the plot or contributes to the mood of the story.
  B. Define what an "epic" is and explain why the *Odyssey* is considered an epic.
  C. Write a character sketch of Odysseus. Include both his strengths and his weaknesses.
  D. Trace the theme of vengeance as it is developed throughout the *Odyssey*.
  E. Discuss the role of Athena in the *Odyssey*. (How would the story be different without her? How does her presence drive the plot along? What does her character reveal about attitudes toward women in Homer's time?)
  F. A classmate who has read neither the Iliad nor the *Odyssey* asks you what some of the differences are between the two. Compare and contrast these two poems.

Creative Reading and Writing: (Choose three.) Let your imagination fly—but include details from the story.

  G. You are Odysseus. Describe the dream you have the night after you escape from the Cyclops.
  H. You are Penelope. Write a poem about what you have going through since your husband left.
  I. You are Agamemnon. Write a letter to Odysseus about how lucky he is to have a wife like Penelope.
  J. You are Antínoüs. Write an interior monologue that reveals your thoughts about Telémachus and that tattered beggar.
  K. You are Athena. Write a letter of recommendation for Odysseus.

Answer Key

Activities #1 and 2: As with other open-ended activities in this packet, there are no right or wrong answers here. Allow students time to share and discuss their responses.

Study Guide

Book I:
1. Odysseus blinded his son, a Cyclops.
2. Athena wanted Zeus to send Hermes with an order for Calypso to let Odysseus go.
3. Suitors pressured Penelope to marry them and squandered Odysseus' wealth.
4. Athena disguised as Méntës suggested he seek information about his father.
5. Laértës was faithful to his wife and careful not to hurt or anger her; other Greek husbands took on mistresses.
6. The prediction questions have no right/wrong answers.

Book II:
1. She had tricked the suitors by promising to marry one when she finished her weaving—then unraveling her work each night.
2. Halithérses was an old Ithacan seer who predicted that Odysseus would return and kill the suitors.
3. Those who failed to defend Odysseus' goods and family were worse than the plotters.
4. She worried that the trip by sea would be dangerous and the suitors would plot his death.

Book III:
1. Agamemnon's wife's lover killed him and was in turn killed by Agamemnon's son.
2. He knew only that Odysseus had not returned home.
3. Nestor thought Meneláus might know about Odysseus.
4. Nestor oversaw the sacrifice of a heifer whose horns had been dipped in gold.

Book IV:
1. Odysseus had come up with a plan for the Greeks to get into the city of Troy by hiding in a wooden horse.
2. The gods had caused a wind to blow him to Egypt.
3. Odysseus was being kept on an island by Calypso.
4. The spirit of Penelope's sister appeared to tell her not to worry about Telémachus because he would return safely.

Book V:
1. She was ordered by Zeus the all-powerful to release Odysseus, so she helped him build a boat.
2. He was probably suspicious of her motives in helping him.
3. Angry Poseidon wanted to keep him from getting home.
4. Athena and a sea nymph helped him stay afloat and get to shore.

Book VI:
1. Athena had given her the idea of washing her wedding clothes.
2. Nausícaa's handmaidens were frightened by the sight of naked, dirty, salty Odysseus.
3. She wished she could have a husband like Odysseus.
4. She told him to go to her mother for help—but to walk with her handmaids instead of riding with her so that the townfolk wouldn't "talk."

Book VII:
1. They were known as skilled sailors.
2. The Phaeácians treated him kindly, offering him food.
3. This wise and generous woman was Nausícaa's mother, Arétë.
4. She recognized the cloak which Nausícaa had given him as one she herself had made.

Book VIII:
1. Demódocus sang about the fate of the Greeks after the Trojan war, the Trojan horse in which the Greeks hid, and the adulterous love of Arës and Aphrodítë.
2. "In truth stranger, you hardly seem like one well used to sport."—p. 150
3. footrace, discuss toss, boxing, jumping, racing, wrestling
4. discuss toss

Book IX:
1. The Cíconës were angry men defending their property and women; several of Odysseus' men were killed.
   The Lotus-Eaters gave the men drug-like fruit; they had to be dragged to the safety of the ship. The Cyclops Polyphémus imprisoned the men in his cave; six were eaten, the rest escaped by ship.
2. They saw his food and wanted to see if he would welcome them.
3. The gift was that Cyclops would eat him last. Odysseus escaped by hiding under one of Polyphémus' rams.
4. He cried out that "No-one" was hurting him since "No-one" is the name that wily Odysseus had given him.

Book X:
1. a bag of winds and instructions not to open it
2. The men greedily opened the bag, releasing a hurricane that blew them back to Aeólia and angering the king of winds by their disobedience.
3. These cannibal giants ate several men.
4. Hermes gave Odysseus the magical mandrake plant to keep Circe from turning him into a pig.

Book XI:
1. Elpénor, his own mother, the seer Tirésias
2. She died of grief when he didn't return after the war.
3. He predicted that Odysseus would get home—but not before undergoing more trials.
4. Agamemnon, Achilles, Ajax

Book XII:
1. The wax would keep them from being lured by the Sirens' song.
2. He had to pass by the monster Scylla and the whirlpool, Charybdis.
3. They disobeyed and ate the sun god's cattle; all died in the shipwreck.
4. Calypso

Book XIII:
1. The Phaeácians brought him home and left him sleeping on the beach with his gifts around him.
2. Poseidon punished them for helping Odysseus; he turned their ship to stone.
3. Athena had brought a mist down on Ithaca.
4. She disguised him as a tattered beggar so that he could make his plans for getting revenge on the suitors—without being recognized.

Book XIV:
1. Eumáeus was the loyal swineherd who despised the arrogant suitors.
2. No, Odysseus told the swineherd a false tale about his past.
3. He wouldn't be surprised if the beggar would lie about having knowledge of Odysseus—in order to get food and a place to stay.
4. He told Eumáeus a story about how Odysseus had once come up with a plan to get him a cloak.

Book XV:
1. Athena went to Sparta and suggested that it was time for Telémachus to return home, lest Penelope decide to marry one of the suitors.
2. Helen interpreted the "sign" of an eagle with a goose in its claws; the fugitive seer interpreted the sign of a hawk plucking feathers from a dove.
3. They planned to arm themselves and attack the suitors.
4. The swineherd, child of wealthy parents, was kidnapped by the slave who cared for him. Eventually Laértës bought him and brought him to Ithaca.

Book XVI:
1. the loyal swineherd, Eumáeus
2. At first he didn't recognize the "suppliant," but Athena advised Odysseus to reveal himself to Telémachus and restored his appearance. In shock for a few moments, Telémachus soon embraced his father.
3. Upon learning of his plans to murder her son, Penelope reminded the arrogant suitor Antínoüs that Odysseus had once saved his father.
4. He claimed that he would protect Telémachus—while plotting his murder.

Book XVII:
1. He was a fugitive seer, in flight after killing a relative. He predicted that Odysseus would have revenge on the suitors.
2. The nasty goatherd insulted him and kicked him.
3. Odysseus' dog died.
4. Antínoüs insulted him and threw a stool at him.

Book XVIII:
1. Irus the pompous beggar didn't want a competitor on his "turf;" he soon saw how muscular Odysseus was.
2. Amphínomus was kind to the "beggar," Odysseus.
3. They gave her brooches, robes, earrings.
4. Odysseus was enraged by Melántho, a shameless, insulting, disloyal handmaid who was seeing one of the suitors.

Book XIX:
1. One of Penelope's handmaids revealed that Penelope was unraveling her weaving each night to put off acting on her promise that she would choose a suitor when she was done with Laértës' shroud.
2. The stranger described some clothing Odysseus had worn long ago—remembered by Penelope.
3. While bathing him, she saw on his leg a scar he had gotten long ago from a boar's tusk.
4. The one who could shoot an arrow through several axheads would win her in marriage.

Book XX:
1. page 404: "How can one man alone assault this crowd...?"
2. He had asked for two signs that he would succeed.
3. The righteous cowherd Philóetius observed sympathetically that the stranger looked noble despite his rags.
4. He was frightened by the omen of the eagle and the dove.

Book XXI:
1. She promised the others she would not marry him.
2. The stranger (Odysseus) was the only one who could even string the bow.
3. the swineherd and the cowherd
4. Odysseus signaled to Telémachus to begin the assault against the suitors.

Book XXII:
1. He was trying to save himself (after seeing Antínoüs killed) by promising to pay Odysseus back.
2. Melánthius fetched the arms from the place where Odysseus and Telémachus had hidden them.
3. Odysseus spared Phémius, the singer, and Medon, the herald who had cared for Telémachus.
4. The disloyal handmaidens were hanged.

Book XXIII:
1. She thought the nurse was mad when she said that Odysseus was back and had slain the suitors.
2. He wanted to put off discovery of the bodies by those who would take revenge.
3. He mentioned details about their bed (which he had carved himself from a tree) that only he would know.
4. He went to the farm to see his father, Laértës.

Book XXIV:
1. Hermes led the dead suitors to Hades.
2. Laértës worried about the vengeance of the dead suitors' families.
3. They wanted to find Odysseus' party and kill them in revenge for the deaths of the suitors.
4. Laértës killed Eupeithes.
5. Athena ordered a stop to the killing—and Zeus threw down a thunderbolt to emphasize the point.

Activity #3
1-b; 2-c; 3-d; 4-g; 5-a; 6-i; 7-h; 8-j; 9-e; 10-f; 11-l; 12-k
(Do not penalize wrong answers, as this is a prereading activity.)
Activity #4
Poseidon, Odysseus, Athena, Zeus, Calypso, Telémachus, Penelope
Activities #5, 6, 7, 8: Personal response.
Activity #9: Answers will vary, but should reflect that Odysseus seems to admire and confide in Athena, above all. He loves his faithful Penelope. He may be attracted to both Calypso and Circe—and even pure and innocent Nausícaa—but cannot forget his wife. He is revolted by wanton Melántho and probably has affection for his faithful nurse, Eurycleia.
Activities #10, 11, 12, 13: Personal response.
Activity #14: I. Homer asks the Muse to help him tell the story of how Odysseus was exiled and lost his men. **II.** Odysseus is being held by Calypso. **III. A.** Nausícaa is like Artemis because both stand out among other women; B,C,D,E,F–Answers will vary. **IV.** 1. land of the Cíconës; 2. land of the lotus-eaters; 3. land of the Cyclops; 4. land of the Laestrygónians; 5. Circe's island; 6. Hades (Accept other accurate answers.) **V.** faced Circe, the cyclops, Scylla and Charybdis; **VI.** Sample answer: Athena steps in to help Odysseus; the Sirens try to lure Odysseus and his men; Zeus helps end the conflict at the end. **VII.** Answers will vary.

Comprehension Quiz, Level 1
Identification: 1-E; 2-C; 3-I; 4-D; 5-G; 6-B; 7-K; 8-L; 9-H; 10-J; 11-A; 12-F
True/False: 13-T; 14-F; 15-F; 16-T; 17-T; 18-T; 19-F; 20-F; 21-F; 22-F; 23-T; 24-T
Matching: 25-g; 26-c; 27-k; 28-b; 29-a; 30-l; 31-f; 32-h; 33-j; 34-i; 35-e; 36-d

Comprehension Quiz, Level 2
Answers should include mention of the fact that—
1. Athena advised Telémachus to call a meeting and order the suitors to leave his house, then go in search of news about his father.
2. Telémachus denounced the suitors.
3. Nestor knew only that Odysseus hadn't returned home.
4. Athena sent the spirit of Penelope's sister to tell her that Telémachus would return safely.

5. Calypso helped him to build a boat, but Poseidon soon capsized it.
6. The daughter of the kind king and queen of the Phaeácians helped feed and clothe him.
7. The king and queen promised to help him get home.
8. Odysseus told the Phaeácians the tale of his travels after the Trojan War.
9. Polyphémus ate six men and Odysseus blinded him.
10. Circe turned the men into swine and kept Odysseus and the men on the island.
11. Tirésias told Odysseus that he would get home—after several more trials—and advised him not to bother the sun god's cattle.
12. The men ate the sun-god's cattle and were all killed at sea as a consequence.

Objective Unit Test, Level 1
Identification: 1-d; 2-j; 3-c; 4-i; 5-f; 6-b; 7-h; 8-g; 9-e; 10-a
Multiple Choice: 11-C; 12-A; 13-B; 14-D; 15-D; 16-A; 17-D; 18-B; 19-A; 20-C; 21-A; 22-B
Fill-Ins: 23-roof; 24-beggar; 25-boat; 26-laundry; 27-bard; 28-dog; 29-cyclops;thunderbolt; 30-loom; 31-cyclops; 32-swine; 33-scar; 34-eagle; 35-bed; 36-axheads; 37-songs; 38-Eurymachus; 39-kill; 40-spared

Short Answer/Essay Unit Test, Level 2
Short Answer:
1. Poseidon turned their ship into stone to punish them for helping Odysseus, who had blinded his son.
2. Athena disguised Odysseus as a beggar so that he could scout out the situation before the suitors captured him.
3. Eumáeus was kidnapped by the slave who cared for him and eventually Laértës bought him and brought him back to Ithaca.
4. Odysseus threw off his disguise with Athena's help so that he could enlist his son's aid in battling the suitors.
5. Melánthius insulted and kicked Odysseus—and was later not only killed, but mutilated.
6. Irus was another beggar who challenged Odysseus to a boxing match which he lost—while entertaining the suitors.
7. While bathing him, Eurycleia recognized a scar he had gotten long ago from a boar's tusk. He told her to keep his secret or he'd kill her.
8. They planned to hide their arms and launch a surprise attack on the men.
9. Penelope said she would marry the suitor who managed to shoot an arrow through a row of axheads; only the stranger (Odysseus) managed it.
10. Odysseus killed the most evil, arrogant suitor first—Antínoüs.
11. Odysseus told his supporters to pretend to be having a wedding feast—to put off the discovery of the bodies and the vengeance that would follow.
12. After the killing started with the death of Eupeithes, Athena called for an end to the bloodshed, Zeus affirmed that idea with a thunderbolt, and a pact was made.
13. **Banner:** Personal response (should reflect knowledge of character and plot)
    Chart:Theme: Answers will vary.

14. Odysseus was wise to think of hiding under the rams, but foolish to give his name.
15. Odysseus was wise to use the wax and to have his men lash him to the mast.
16. Odysseus was foolish to forget what Tirésias had said about not arming himself—and lost several men to Scylla as a result.
17. Odysseus was wise not to open the bag, but his men were foolish and greedy to open it.
18. Odysseus was wise to counsel the men not to touch the cattle and the men were foolish to ignore that counsel.

Quote Identification
19. Speaker: Odysseus 20. was saying that he left Troy and went to the land of the Cíconës to pillage their goods and kill their men.
21. Speaker: Telémachus 22. is saying that he would like to put an end to the suitors' abuse, but he feels that he lacks the power.
23. Speaker: Penelope 24. is telling Odysseus not to be angry with her for being skeptical about her identity—that fate has kept them apart for a long time and now has put them back together.
25. Speaker: Agamemnon 26. is saying that his wife and her lover killed him before he could see his son again after the war.
27. Speaker: Athena 28. is telling Odysseus that he must stop fighting the suitors' families now before he makes Zeus angry.

Essay
A. Three settings students might choose include Calypso's caves—and how they became Odysseus' prison; Hades—and how his visit there developed the idea of his "death" and "rebirth; and the Cyclops' cave—and how Odysseus learned an important lesson about the dangers of being arrogant, there.
B. Students should mention some of these: invocation to the Muse, in media res, Homeric similes, expansive setting.
C. Strengths include his courage and brains and quest for adventure; weaknesses include his pride and occasional foolhardiness
D. Answers should mention Poseidon's revenge against Odysseus; Odysseus' revenge against the suitors; Agamemnon's son's revenge against his father's murderer
E. Answers should touch on Athena as the embodiment of the "ideal woman."
F. Three points of contrast include the fact that the Iliad covers only a few days and the *Odyssey*, 19 years; the Iliad is a series of accounts of battle while the *Odyssey* tells of one man's attempt to return home; there is much more of the supernatural in the *Odyssey*.

Creative Reading and Writing: Personal response.